This book belongs to

Annie

Morrow

This edition published by Parragon Books Ltd in 2016

Parragon Books Ltd
Chartist House
15–17 Trim Street
Bath BA1 1HA, UK
www.parragon.com

ISBN 978-1-4748-7824-1

Printed in China

Bath · New York · Cologne · Melbourne · Delhi
Hong Kong · Shenzhen · Singapore

Dory was a little blue tang. She lived with her parents in a beautiful coral cave surrounded by sea grass.

From a very young age, Dory had trouble remembering things.

"Hi, I'm Dory," she would say when she met someone new, and then she would tell them that she had short-term memory loss.

Dory's parents worried about their forgetful daughter and did everything they could to stop her from getting lost. But, one day, Dory got separated from her parents and couldn't find her way back home. Before long, she was lost and alone.

It was getting dark, so Dory swam under a rock and tried to sleep.

"Just keep swimming, just keep swimming," she sang quietly to herself as she closed her eyes.

Dory just kept on swimming and swimming, getting further and further away from her home.

The time passed and Dory grew up, but she still asked every fish she met if they had seen her parents. None of them had.

"Hi, I've lost my family," Dory would say. "Can you help me?"

"Where did you see them last?" the fish would ask.

"Well ... uh. Funny story, but, uh ... I forgot."

Poor Dory had forgotten where she came from and why she was lost.

One day while Dory was swimming along, she looked up and saw a boat speed by. Just then, she swam headfirst into a clownfish, who was yelling something about his son, Nemo.

"They took him away!" the clownfish cried. "I have to find the boat!"

"A boat?" said Dory. "Hey, I've seen a boat!"

Dory and the clownfish, whose name was Marlin, swam off towards the boat in search of Nemo....

One year later, long after Marlin and Dory had brought Nemo back home, the three friends still lived together on the coral reef. They had a happy and colourful home, and had lots of fun together.

Sometimes Dory would swim away on her own, so Marlin and Nemo had to keep a close eye on her.

Dory was very happy and had forgotten to ask for help to find her parents. Marlin and Nemo were all the family she needed.

One day, Nemo's school teacher, Mr Ray, took his class to watch the stingrays migrating back home. Dory went along as a teaching assistant. It was a wonderful sight – hundreds of stingrays flapping their huge wings and singing as they swam. Dory was amazed.

Mr Ray warned his class not to get too close to the stingrays, because their flapping caused a strong current in the water called an undertow. The undertow could sweep any little fish away.

But in her amazement, Dory forgot Mr Ray's warning.
She swam too close to the stingrays and, before anybody
could help, she was swept away in the undertow!

Dory's world spun around her and then faded to black.

When Dory opened her eyes, Nemo, Mr Ray and the students were peering down at her. Mr Ray told the children to give Dory some room.

As her eyes fluttered open, Dory quietly murmured something under her breath. Only Nemo heard it.

"The Jewel of Morro Bay, California?" Nemo repeated.

Later, back home, Nemo reminded Dory what she had muttered as she was waking up. It took Dory a moment to realize what it meant, but suddenly she knew – the Jewel of Morro Bay was her home! She remembered her parents!

"My family!" Dory cried. "I remember my family!"

All these sudden memories
sent Dory into a spin. She swam
straight to the edge of the reef.
Marlin and Nemo chased after her.
"I have a family!" Dory called back
to them. "They don't know where I am.
Let's go!"

"Dory, California's all the way across
the ocean," said Marlin.

Dory stopped swimming and looked back at her friends.

"Please," she said. "All I know ... is that I miss them. I didn't know what that felt like. Do you know what that feels like?"

Marlin looked at Nemo, the son he once lost across the ocean.

"Yes," said Marlin. "I know what that feels like."

"Please, Marlin," said Dory. "I can't find them on my own. I'll forget. Please help me find my family."

"Yeah, Dad," added Nemo. "You can get us all the way across the ocean, right?"

"No," answered Marlin, sighing. "But I know a guy...."

Marlin, Nemo and Dory hitched a ride across the ocean with their old friend, Crush the turtle. When they arrived in Morro Bay, they found themselves surrounded by rubbish.

"This feels familiar," said Dory.

Dory suddenly remembered
something else – when she had first
lost her parents, she had asked the
crabs that lived here for help.

Just then, a giant squid appeared out of nowhere
and chased Marlin, Nemo and Dory! The trio swam
as fast as they could to escape.

After they had escaped the clutches of the squid, Marlin was upset. Nemo had almost been badly hurt. Dory tried to comfort Nemo, but in his moment of worry, Marlin snapped at her.

"Go wait over there and forget," Marlin said. "It's what you do best."

Dory was sad that she had upset Marlin. She was determined to make it up to him, so she swam off to look for help.

Just then, Dory heard a loud voice in the distance, saying: "Welcome to the Marine Life Institute, where we believe in Rescue, Rehabilitation and Release."

Dory swam to the surface and Marlin and Nemo caught up with her.

"Guys! I found help!" Dory cried.

"Look out!" yelled Marlin, as a boat appeared behind Dory. She was scooped up by a human and carried away!

"Don't worry, Dory!" a panicked Marlin called after her. "Stay calm! We'll come and find you!"

The next thing Dory knew, she had a tag clipped to her fin and was dropped into a tank. Suddenly, an octopus appeared. He had one tentacle missing – he was a 'septopus'! He reached one of his long tentacles towards Dory.

"Name's Hank," he said.

Hank explained that Dory was in Quarantine, and the tag was a transport tag – it meant she was going to an aquarium in Cleveland.

"Cleveland!" gasped Dory. "No, I can't go to the Cleveland! I have to get to the Jewel of Morro Bay, California...."

"That's this place," said Hank. "The Marine Life Institute. The Jewel of Morro Bay, California. You're here."

Hank wanted Dory's orange tag, so that he could go and live on his own in a glass tank in Cleveland. He didn't like living with other fish.

Dory explained that she needed to find her parents. So Hank grumpily agreed to a deal – he would help Dory and then she would give him the tag. Hank scooped Dory up into a water-filled coffee pot and they set off.

Hank carried Dory to a map
of the MLI (the Marine Life
Institute). Dory spotted a purple
shell on the map, which caused
another memory to pop into
her head. She remembered
that her mother had loved
purple shells!

Dory remembered collecting shells as a child. Her parents had used the shells to make a path, to lead Dory back home if she ever got lost.

Dory snapped out of her memory and saw an MLI staff member walking by, carrying a bucket. Hank hid, but Dory read the word on the bucket – it said 'DESTINY'.

Suddenly, Dory felt it was very important that she get into that bucket – so she did! Hank followed as fast as he could as she was carried away.

Dory was tipped from the bucket into a large pool and Hank followed close behind. The pool was home to a giant whale shark called Destiny, who couldn't see very well and often swam into walls. Her neighbour was a beluga whale called Bailey – he was at the MLI because he had bumped his head. He thought he had lost his echolocation ability, which helped him to see things that were far away.

Destiny realized that she had known Dory when they were young! Dory had lived in the Open Ocean exhibit and they used to talk to each other through the pipes.

Dory had to get to the Open Ocean exhibit – she was sure that's where her parents would be!

On their way to the Open Ocean exhibit, Dory led Hank in the wrong direction and they ended up in a 'touch pool'. Small and grabby hands came at them from above. It was terrifying!

Hank hid under a rock and wouldn't come out.

"I'm sorry, Hank," said Dory. "I'm sorry I can't remember right."

Just then, Dory remembered that she had once said the same thing to her parents. Her mother had said that Dory didn't need to be sorry.

"You know what you need to do?" Dory's mother had said. "Just ... keep swimming."

"Hank, we've just got to keep swimming!" Dory cried.

But Hank still didn't want to move.

"I know you're scared," said Dory, "but you can't give up. Follow me!"

Dory grabbed Hank's tentacle and they raced across the touch pool. But one of the children poked Hank. This caused his octopus ink to ooze out and turn the whole pool black! The kids all shouted in shock and ran away. Hank and Dory weren't in danger any more.

"Wow," said Hank, stunned. "Y-you ... got us out of there."

Meanwhile, outside in the bay, Marlin and Nemo had met a bird called Becky, who carried them into the MLI inside a bucket. Marlin was terrified, but he knew it was the only way to find Dory.

Inside the MLI, before reaching the exhibits, Becky spotted some spilled popcorn on the ground. She left Marlin and Nemo hanging on a tree branch and flew down for a feed!

Marlin nudged the bucket forwards until the branch pulled under the weight and the two fish were flung into a tank at the gift shop! They didn't know what to do next. They were very worried about Dory.

"She would definitely have an idea of what to do if she were here," said Marlin. "I don't know how she does that."

"I don't think she knows, Dad," said Nemo. "She just ... *does*."

Marlin knew that Nemo was right.

"What would Dory do?" asked Nemo.

Marlin realized that Dory would simply look at the first thing she saw and.... Just then, Marlin spotted a line of water jets leading to an outdoor pool exhibit. He sighed.

"Dory would do it," Nemo said with a smile.

With that, father and son leaped towards the water jets. Each jet propelled them on to the next, until they landed safely in the exhibit. They made it!

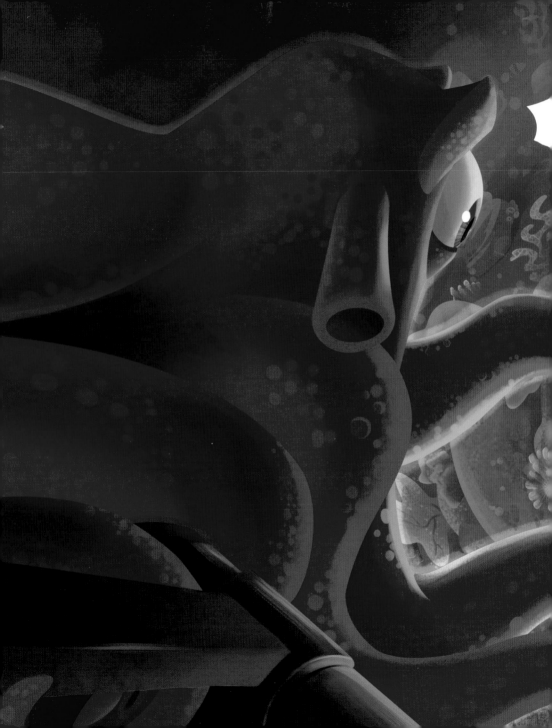

At that moment, Hank and Dory had finally reached the Open Ocean exhibit.

Dory couldn't believe she was about to meet her parents. She turned to Hank.

"They're actually down there, aren't they? I hope I can find them."

"Knowing you," said Hank, "I'm liking your chances. Now go get your family."

With that, Dory gave Hank her transport tag and Hank dropped her into the water.

Dory swam down through the clear, cool tank. At the bottom, she spotted a trail of shells, just like the ones she remembered from her childhood. This was her home!

Just then, Dory saw a purple shell near an entrance to a pipe. She remembered that her parents had warned her not to go near the pipe, as the strong undertow could carry her away.

Dory remembered with a shock that she had tried to collect
this purple shell for her mother, and been sucked into the pipe!
"It was my fault," Dory whispered.
"My parents ... I lost them."

Dory didn't know what to do next. This was her home, but there were no blue tangs here!

A small crab told Dory that all the blue tangs had been taken to Quarantine, ready to be shipped to the aquarium in Cleveland.

"What? No!" cried Dory. "But I ... I just got here!"

The crab told Dory that it was easy to get to Quarantine, through the pipes. "It's two lefts and a right," the crab said.

Dory looked at the pipe entrance, gathered her courage and squeezed through the grate into the darkness.

"Okay," she told herself. "I can do this. Two lefts and a right."

But before long, Dory forgot how many lefts she had already taken. She was lost. She began to panic, but then she remembered her friends, Destiny and Bailey – she could call to them through the pipes!

"Destineeeeeee!" Dory called in her best whale voice.

"Dory?" a voice answered. It was Destiny!

Destiny had an idea – Bailey could use
his echolocation to find Dory and give her directions.
He just had to make an 'ooo' sound, and echoes would come
back to him from far away. It was like seeing a picture in his head.
Bailey still believed his echolocation was broken, but Destiny soon
convinced him to try. After a few attempts, it finally worked. He could
see Dory and the whole pipe system! He began to give Dory directions.

Dory followed Bailey's
directions – and bumped
straight into Marlin and Nemo!
They had swum into the pipes
to search for their friend.

"You found me!" Dory cried.

Marlin wanted them all to head home, but Dory stopped him.

"My parents are here," she said.

"You found your parents?" Nemo asked, amazed.

Dory explained everything that had happened, and the three of them made their way towards Quarantine. The journey was much easier now that Dory had some company!

Dory, Marlin and Nemo made it to Quarantine and leaped into one of the tanks. They saw with a shock that the tank of blue tangs had already been loaded on the truck to Cleveland.

Suddenly, Hank appeared.

"Hank, we need to get in that tank," said Dory. "That rhymed!"

Hank lifted Dory, Marlin and Nemo into a coffee pot and put them into the tank on the truck.

The other blue tangs recognized Dory, but they had sad news. Dory's parents had left the Open Ocean exhibit and come to Quarantine years ago – nobody knew where they were now!

Dory was heartbroken. She drifted slowly back into the waiting coffee pot. Hank scooped it up and backed out of the truck.

Hank looked down into the coffee pot.

"Where's everybody else?" he asked.

Marlin and Nemo were still inside the truck! Before Hank could do anything else, a member of MLI staff grabbed him! The coffee pot fell to the floor. Dory spilled into a drain, which took her out of the MLI and back into the ocean. Once again, Dory was alone and lost.

In the bay outside the MLI, Dory swam through the water with no idea what to do. She began to panic. She was scared that she would forget everybody again.

But then Dory spotted something. It was a trail of shells. Dory liked shells, so she followed the trail.

Just then, two shapes emerged from the darkness. It was her parents!

Dory's parents had been creating shell pathways all this time, in the hope that Dory would see them and remember!

"It's you! It's really you!" cried Dory as she burst into tears.

"Oh, honey, you found us," said Dory's mum. "And you know why you found us? Because you remembered. You remembered in your own, amazing, Dory way."

Dory was so happy to be back with her family again, but she suddenly remembered Marlin and Nemo. She had to go back and save them!

Dory and her parents rushed towards the MLI walls, but saw, with horror, that the truck was pulling away! Marlin and Nemo were inside.

Dory swam round in a panic, trying to think of a plan. Suddenly she remembered her friends, Destiny and Bailey. They could help!

"DESTINEEEEEE!" Dory called in her whale voice.

"Dory?" Destiny answered.

Bailey used his echolocation and saw that Dory was just outside the MLI. The two whales leaped over the wall and into the open ocean to help their little friend.

Bailey used his echolocation to look for the truck. The friends raced after it and caught up just before a bridge.

Dory had an idea. They had to stop the traffic, so she asked some nearby otters to climb up onto the bridge – and cuddle! The sight of the cute otters made the drivers, including the truck driver, come skidding to a halt.

Destiny used her tail to flip Dory up towards the bridge. An otter caught Dory, opened the truck back doors and put her inside. The plan had worked!

Inside the truck, Dory was surprised
to see Hank – he had sneaked on board!
He lifted Dory into the tank with Marlin
and Nemo.

"You came back!" cried Nemo.

"Of course," Dory said.
"I couldn't leave my family."

But just then, Destiny
called from the ocean to
tell Dory that the
traffic at the front
of the hold-up
was starting to
move again.

Marlin had a plan. He called to Becky, who arrived and
scooped Marlin and Nemo into her bucket.

"No, no, wait!" cried Marlin. "We don't have Dory!"

But Becky didn't stop. She dropped Marlin and Nemo
into the ocean. Marlin told Becky to go back and get Dory,
so she headed back to the truck.

In the ocean, Marlin and Nemo met Destiny and Bailey.
Then Marlin spotted the two blue tangs with them and was
amazed – they were Dory's parents!

Becky landed in the truck and Hank reached for Dory to
put her in the bucket. But Dory stopped him.

"You're not going to Cleveland," she said. "You're coming
to the ocean with me."

Hank wasn't sure at first, but Dory soon convinced him that
living with friends was much better than being alone in a tank.

But, just then, the driver slammed the back doors shut.
Dory, Hank and Becky were trapped inside!

Hank slipped out of the truck
through a vent and spread himself
across the windshield. The shocked driver
pulled over and got out. Hank climbed into the
driver's seat and locked the doors!
Hank grabbed Dory from the tank and plopped
her into a cup of water on the dashboard.
Then, as the driver yelled from the side of
the road, Hank started to drive the truck!

"Hank," said Dory. "I'm going to ask you to do something crazy."

Hank smiled. He knew what to do.

Back in the water, Dory's family watched as Hank drove the truck off the bridge and into the ocean!

The doors flew open and all the fish spilled out into the waves. They were free!

Marlin, Nemo and Dory headed back home across the ocean – and they took all their new family and friends with them!

Hank, Destiny, Bailey and Dory's parents all lived together in their new home.

Dory was happier than she had ever been. She could now swim off on her own sometimes, because she always remembered how to get back to her huge family.

"I'll see you in a while guys," Dory said one day. "I've got something I wanna do."

But Marlin still worried that Dory would
get lost, so he followed her. He stayed a good
distance behind so that Dory wouldn't see him.
He watched as she swam to the edge of the reef
and looked out at the ocean.

"Hey, Marlin," said Dory. She somehow
knew he was there.

"Oh," said Marlin. "Hello Dory."

Marlin joined Dory and they gazed out into
the blue.

"Wow. It really is quite a view," said Marlin.

"Yup," replied Dory.

"So is this one," Marlin said as he turned
round and saw that everyone else had followed
Dory, too.

Dory looked back at her whole family
and smiled.

"Unforgettable," she said.